A SPEED BUMP & SLINGSHOT
MISADVENTURE

NIGHT
OF THE
LIVING
ZOMBIE BUGS

Dave Coverly

Christy Ottaviano Books

Henry Holt and Company ✦ New York

Thanks to Nathan Fowle for the very inspiring
Giant Zombie Fly with One Eye drawing!

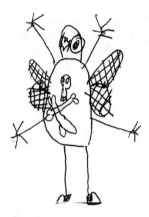

Henry Holt and Company, *Publishers since 1866*
175 Fifth Avenue, New York, NY 10010
mackids.com

Henry Holt® is a registered trademark of Macmillan Publishing Group, LLC.
Copyright © 2017 by Dave Coverly

Library of Congress Cataloging-in-Publication Data
Names: Coverly, Dave, author, illustrator.
Title: Night of the living zombie bugs / Dave Coverly.
Description: First edition. | New York : Henry Holt and Company, 2017. | Series: A Speed Bump & Slingshot
misadventure ; [3] | "Christy Ottaviano Books." | Summary: Now that they are Eagle Scouts, Speed Bump and
Slingshot must summon the courage to face the zombie bugs infesting their forest.
Identifiers: LCCN 2017002415 (print) | LCCN 2017030597 (ebook) | ISBN 9781250114013 (Ebook) | ISBN
9781250114006 (hardcover)
Subjects: | CYAC: Birds—Fiction. | Best friends—Fiction. | Friendship—Fiction. | Zombies—Fiction. | Cicadas—
Fiction. | Humorous stories.
Classification: LCC PZ7.1.C684 (ebook) | LCC PZ7.1.C684 Nm 2017 (print) | DDC [Fic]—dc23
LC record available at https://lccn.loc.gov/2017002415

ISBN 978-1-250-11400-6 (hardback)

Our books may be purchased in bulk for promotional, educational, or business use. Please contact your local
bookseller or the Macmillan Corporate and Premium Sales Department at (800) 221-7945 ext. 5442 or by
e-mail at MacmillanSpecialMarkets@macmillan.com.

First edition, 2017
Printed in the United States of America by
LSC Communications, Harrisonburg, Virginia
1 3 5 7 9 10 8 6 4 2

For my daughters, Alayna and Simone,

sisters who are also best friends.

Don't miss these other books by Dave Coverly:

Night of the Living Worms:
A Speed Bump and Slingshot Misadventure, Book 1

Night of the Living Shadows:
A Speed Bump and Slingshot Misadventure, Book 2

Dogs Are People, Too:
A Collection of Cartoons to Make Your Tail Wag

The Very Inappropriate Word,
written by Jim Tobin

Sue MacDonald Had a Book,
written by Jim Tobin

CONTENTS

"It's Speed Bump! I can't wake him up! None of my usual tricks worked, not even taking off his headphones and yelling at him!"

"Did you try tipping over his nest?"

"Yes!" Slingshot cried. "I tried EVERYTHING!

"Oh, I hope he's not..." Slingshot couldn't even bring himself to finish that thought, it was so horrible.

"That DOES sound serious. Quick, Slingshot, follow me to my brother's hole in the tree!"

The pair flew through the forest as fast as their wings would take them.

Inside Speed Bump's room was a terrifying scene.

Early Bird got a very solemn look on his face. He turned to Slingshot, put a wing on his shoulder, and said, "This is not good, not good at all. If Speed Bump is a zombie, it means other birds are turning into zombies, too."

Slingshot gasped and chewed his wing feathers.

"In fact, this zombie plague may have spread as far as Africa by now. Have you ever seen a zombie parrot? It's not a pretty sight." Early Bird paused. "Well, I take that back. Parrots are really colorful, so they're still a pretty sight. But you catch my drift."

"Holy crow, what if the plague has spread all the way to Antarctica?" Slingshot asked.

"There could be terrifying zombie penguins there already! Okay, maybe not too terrifying because they're usually so cute!"

"And hummingbirds!" Early Bird continued. "Zombie hummingbirds would be so fast! Then again, they're tiny, right? Seriously, we could just knock them aside with our wings, no problem."

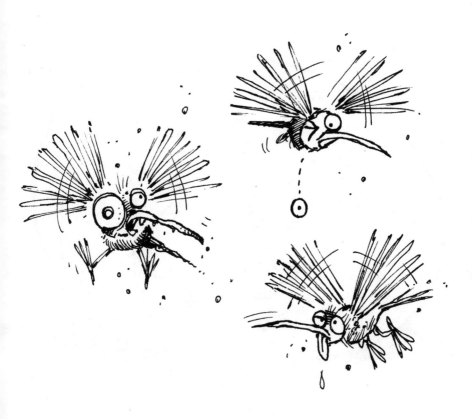

Early Bird burst out laughing.

"Slingshot, buddy, I'm kidding! My brother's just sleepwalking. He's been doing it since he was a chick. I'll bet he even wandered around inside his egg before he hatched!"

Slingshot looked wary. "So...no zombie pigeons, either?"

"No zombie ANYTHING. Watch, I'll show you the trick to wake him up when he's like this."

Early Bird slowly lifted one of Speed Bump's tiny wings and tickled underneath it. Speed Bump stopped groaning. His body began to shake and his little tail started to twitch. One eye opened, then the other. His beak moved but no sound came out.

Suddenly Speed Bump was rolling
around on the floor, gasping out
squeaky little laughs. Then he stopped,
sat up, and looked toward the hole in
the tree.

"Word of warning if you ever try this," Early Bird said, "tickling wakes him up, but it also makes him tinkle."

"Call me Squishymeal," said Slingshot as he dropped a juicy bug into his mouth.

"What?" Speed Bump said, looking over his shoulder. He was kicking berries toward a hole in the Sycamore tree. "Do you really give insects names before you eat them?"

"Sometimes."

20

The bird buddies hopped off the branch and glided through the trees together.

You scared me this morning, *mon ami*. I thought you turned into a zombie!

Slingshot, you know there are no such things as ZOMBIES, right?

"How do you know? Maybe there are!" Slingshot shuddered at the thought. "Zombie ostriches. Ugh."

"Have you ever seen a zombie?"

"No. But I'd never seen an evil Nightcrawler before, or a mouse that burps, or a mall full of shadows, or a bird that lives in a trash can, or—"

"Okay, Okay, I get it. That's not the same, though," Speed Bump sighed.

"Maybe not, but the finch twins said they heard from the potoo, who heard from the oriole, who heard from the sparrow's third cousin that the old fortune-teller rook on the far side of the forest has seen zombies."

The rook? I heard she's creepy, all right, but that doesn't mean she's seen ZOMBIES.
WAIT— maybe she IS a zombie!
OOOOOOOOOOOOo!
Okay, okay, Mr. Funnyfeathers, but it COULD be true.

They flapped and bobbed, eating the occasional bug out of the air and swooping down to Speed Bump's favorite berry bush. Slingshot was munching and making little happy noises, juice dribbling down his chin, when he suddenly stopped.

"Speedy, what's that?"

Speed Bump rolled his eyes. "NOW what? Why are you so jumpy today?"

Slingshot pointed to the ground. A mound of gray fur was sticking out from the other side of the bush. There was a long, pink tail, and four feet with curved, sharp claws.

"Sshhh," whispered Speed Bump.

"Let's get out of here."

"No, wait, it's not moving. Let's peek over the top."

Slingshot squeaked and covered his beak. "It's a possum! Look at its scary, pointed face and little fangs! Those fang things freak me out!"

Shh! It's still not moving! I think there's something wrong with it.
Maybe it's sleeping. We should let it sleep. That would be the NICE thing to do. I say we go home and let it rest in peace.

Speed Bump flew down near the possum, being careful not to stand too close.

Hello? Are you okay, Mr. Possum?

It didn't move.

"Slingshot! I think it might be...might be...dead!"

Slingshot stood behind his friend.

Speed Bump poked the possum gently with a stick. It didn't move. He poked it harder. It still didn't move. He poked it a few more times, just to be sure.

31

"It's gone. That's so sad."

The friends sighed and Slingshot put his arm around his buddy.

Suddenly, the possum jumped to its feet. The birds screamed, and Speed Bump leaped into Slingshot's arms. The possum glared at them with its narrow eyes and hissed.

SSSSSS

Then, with a flick of its bald tail, the possum ambled off toward the forest, grumbling as it shook the dirt off its fur.

Slingshot dropped Speed Bump.

CHAPTER TWO
'FRAIDY BIRDS

We were sitting on a bush!
Then we SAW something!
It was furry and gray and REALLY BIG!
And STINKY!
Yeah, STINKY!
It was a POSSUM!
P.U.!

"**A**re you sure it wasn't just, you know, sleeping?" Early Bird asked.

"No way!" Speed Bump said. "We poked it really hard! No one could sleep through that!"

"Well, boys, I don't know what to tell you," Early Bird said. He bit off half of the worm he'd gotten that morning and tossed the other half to a drooling Slingshot. "But I think you'd better sleep with one eye open tonight, in case that ZOMBIE POSSUM COMES TO GET YOU!"

"Very funny," Speed Bump said,
looking nervously out the door. "Come
on, Slingshot, let's go."

Speed Bump and Slingshot could
hear Early Bird laughing as they
flew away.

"I don't care what your brother
says, I know what we saw," Slingshot
said as they soared over the forest.
The sky had a faint orange glow from
the setting sun. "I'm never going to fall
asleep tonight!"

"Yeah, my tail feathers are still
shaking."

"You know what we should do?"

"Stop letting our imaginations run wild?"

"No, *mon ami*. We should have a slumber party so we're not so scared."

"Great idea! Let's get Hoover and Soda Pop!"

They flew off into the dusk to find their friends, listening for little mousy burps and hoping Hoover would be done sleeping for the day. Nighttime was pretty scary without him.

CHAPTER THREE

BFFS

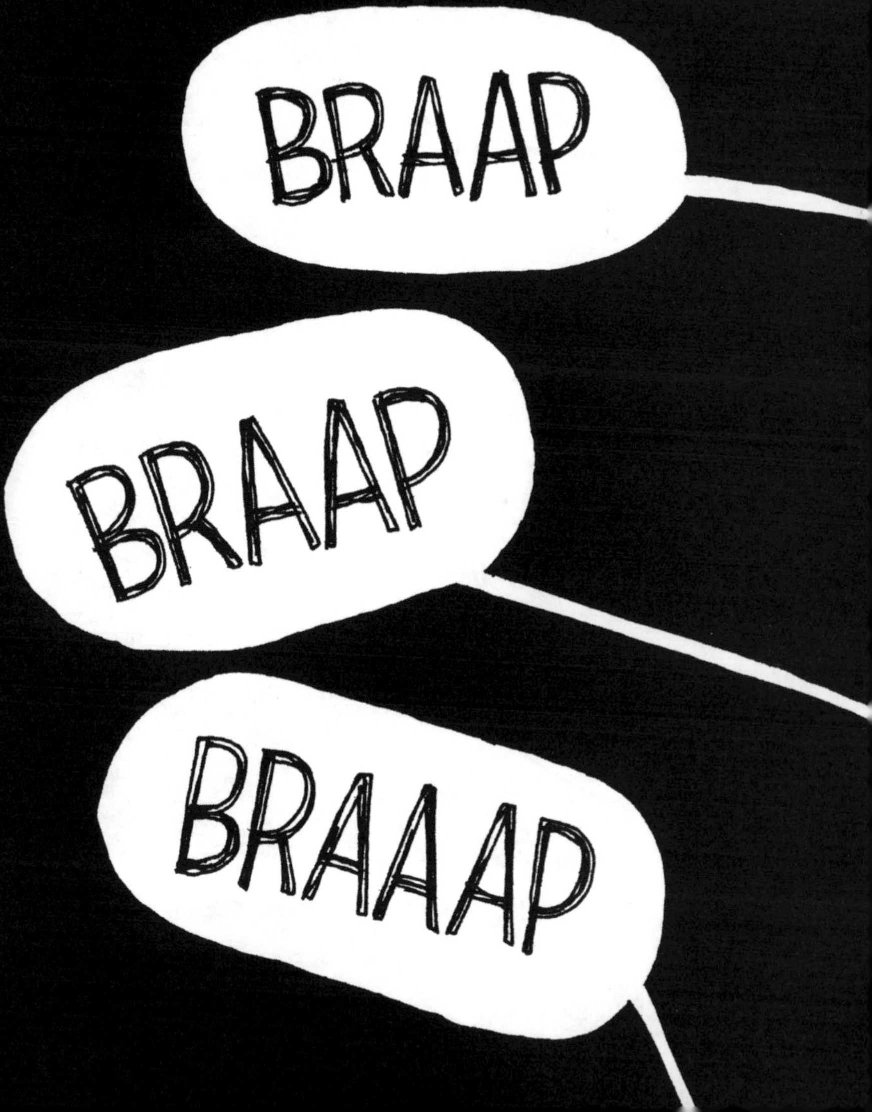

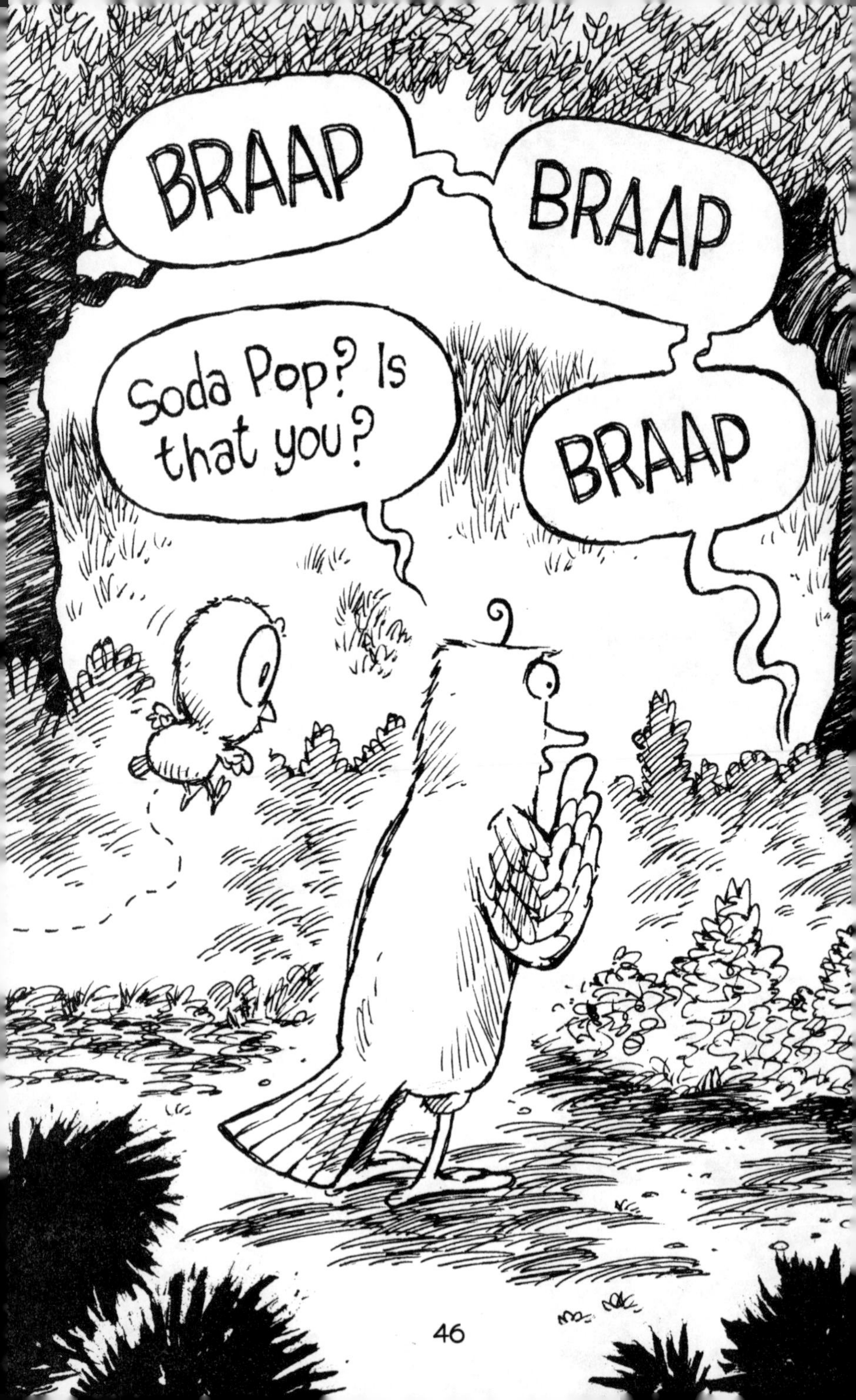
BRAAP
BRAAP
Soda Pop? Is that you?
BRAAP

"BRRAAAP!"

"Oh, sorry, we thought you were someone else. You don't happen to know a burping mouse, do you?"

"You mean Soda Pop? Everyone knows Soda Pop." The bird buddies looked at each other with surprise—not because the bullfrog knew the mouse's name, but because her voice was soft and pretty.

"Yeah, that's him! We're trying to track him down, but the forest is huge."

"Sounds like you two need a BFF."

Slingshot looked puzzled. "'Best Friends Forever'? We already are!"

"No, silly. 'Bullfrog Friend Finder.'"

She let out another loud "brraaap," and suddenly the forest was echoing with other bullfrogs "braaping" and "blurking" and "barrooging" from their hiding places inside old logs and under the plant life.

It was silent for a moment, and then there was a rustling behind them.

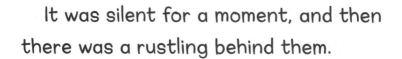

BUUUUUUUURRRP

Soda Pop came around a tree, his whiskers still quivering from the burp.

"My feathered friends! Look at you two, being brave and coming into the forest at night again!"

After the hugs and high fives and bonjours, they turned to thank the bullfrog, but she was gone. They heard a small splash in the distance.

"We came to invite you to a slumber party at Speed Bump's place!" Slingshot said as he snatched a mosquito out of the air.

"A slumber party? Tonight? That sounds fun and sort of, um, sudden."

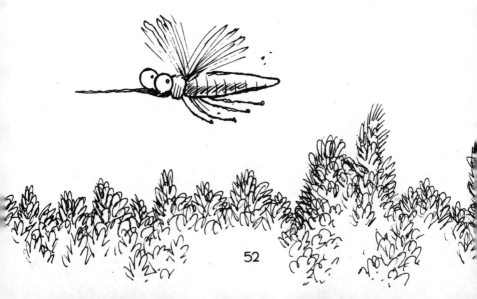

The birds told their mouse buddy about the possum and how it didn't move and how many times they poked it—hard!—and about the dirt on its fur and its evil glare, and then they told him about the old fortune teller rook and how everyone KNOWS she's seen zombies and so they must be real.

Soda Pop took a deep breath. The full moon had slipped out from behind the evening clouds, making his gray face appear to glow. Speed Bump and Slingshot couldn't believe what he said next:

It's TRUE.

57

"It's even worse than you think," Soda Pop whispered, holding on to his tail. "I hear she says there are zombies *in this forest.*"

Just as the word *zombies* came out of Soda Pop's mouth, a huge shadow flew over them all.

Speed Bump jumped into Slingshot's arms.

CHAPTER FOUR
A ROOK IN A
CROOKED TREE

Hoover landed behind the group with a soft flutter of his giant wings.

"No, it's true! My chipmunk friend heard it from a skunk who heard it from a bat who heard it from a raccoon on the other side of the forest!"

Cheesable mercy! What do we do?
There's only one thing TO do. We need to visit that old rook and stop this PREPOSTEROUS rumor. All this zombie talk is just SILLY!

After thinking it over for a few minutes, they agreed. It was always wise to listen to Hoover.

The three of them huddled together on the owl's back and were lifted into the night sky.

"I feel safer up here," Speed Bump said, looking over the side.

"Yep. No zombies in the sky!" Soda Pop agreed.

"But what if there are zombie flying squirrels?" Slingshot wondered.

Hoover rolled his enormous eyes and turned his head all the way around to face them. "THERE ARE NO...Listen, you guys just need to relax, okay? See that ridge? The rook lives in an ancient pine tree on the other side. Just talk about something less scary than zombies until we get there."

Nightcrawlers?

Ghosts?

Girls?

They were quiet the rest of the
way. Speed Bump fell asleep for a few
minutes, and Slingshot nibbled on a few
fleas he found underneath Hoover's
feathers.

"There it is."

Hoover pointed to a tall, scraggly pine tree that stuck out above the others. It looked like a crooked finger, bent as if to say, *This way, if you dare*. Soda Pop managed a squeaky little burp. Speed Bump and Slingshot gulped loudly.

As they flew closer, they could see
a hole in the top of the swaying pine.
It was the shape of a bird's eye, and it
glowed yellow. Hoover lifted his massive
wings and coasted down onto a branch
just below it.

"All right, my fretful friends, here's your chance to find out about zombies once and for all."

"I have butterflies in my stomach," Speed Bump said.

"I WISH I had butterflies in my stomach," Slingshot said. "Mmm, butterflies..."

"I'm having second thoughts," Soda Pop squeaked.

"Don't make me turn myself around and take you all home!" Hoover said. "Go on in. The old rook might look creepy, but I hear she's harmless."

They peered through the hole, their eyes adjusting to the bright glow from inside.

"Whoa," all three said in unison.

The room was full of jars of fireflies balanced on bent shelves. They glowed on old tables and all over the floor, too. Hanging from the ceiling were strings with colorful feathers on them. In all the nooks and crannies were sticks put together in weird patterns, pinecones pecked into animal shapes, bits of aluminum and yarn, and a few odd things none of them had ever seen before.

Then the shadow of a bird rose up in the back of the room, as if growing from the floor! Above its long, pointy beak was a strangely pointed head, and the bird flowed toward them, as if floating on a breeze. Its voice sounded like two dry branches rubbing against each other.

CHAPTER FIVE
A SQUAB STORY

"**H**ow do I know your names, you wonder? I know all. I see all. You're here because you have a question about..." The old rook leaned toward them and raised one eyebrow. "ZOMBIES!"

"Yes!" Speed Bump exclaimed. "Do they really exist? HAVE YOU SEEN THEM?"

"You might want to sit down for this, my young friends."

TSE·TSE FLY WINGS

WORM OIL

BAT BOOGERS

LIZARD TOENAILS

URP.

They sat in a semicircle in front of
her on spongy mushroom tops.

These are so comfy on my tushy! Do you think she'd let me take one home?

Focus, buddy.

The old rook bent down and looked
them in the eye.

"Yes, zombies are real."

The friends gasped.

"And yes, I have seen them myself!"

"I KNEW IT!" Slingshot croaked.

A faraway look came over the rook's eyes. "When I was a squab—a baby rook—my grandmother told me tales about the zombie creatures that would come out of the earth. 'Every seventeen years,' she said, 'they emerge from the dirt in the thousands, their large red eyes staring through you, their loud screams making your blood feel as cold as a penguin egg.'"

"Of course, I didn't believe her. 'What a silly story,' I said! So she took me to the edge of the forest one night, just before dawn, so that I would know. I saw them myself, the hideous beasts still covered in dirt, rising from the dead and crawling out of their holes in the ground!"

They all gasped.

"That's when I realized: The world is a very strange and mysterious place indeed!"

The friends were speechless. Then the rook said: "And this is what I need to tell you—that was seventeen years ago TONIGHT."

"NO!" Speed Bump and Slingshot said, huddling together. Soda Pop shivered as if a cold wind had passed through him.

"Are you just trying to scare us?" the mouse asked.

"If you don't believe me, take this and see for yourself!"

"What is it?" Speed Bump whimpered.

"A Zombie Map! You'll never find them without it."

"Because they're underground?"

"Yes. But also because you four are terrible with directions."

"How did you—oh, right, you know all."

"If you dare go, remember this: Do not look directly at them. Their eyes are huge and red and will freeze you with fear. Brrr." The rook shook all over and adjusted her head scarf.

Good luck to you all!

And be careful. Be very, very careful.

CHAPTER SIX

LET'S GET READY TO RUMBLE!

"**N**ew plan—we should fly home and go to bed," said Soda Pop. "Zombies! Ugh. Who needs 'em!"

"Maybe," said Speed Bump. "But what if that old rook is just crazy? What if we find out zombies DON'T exist? Then we can stop being scared!"

"Yeah, we have to know. Besides,

Hoover will protect us!" Slingshot said, his face buried in the Zombie Map. "By the way, why does it say NEWS on here? Is this news?"

"Those letters stand for North, East, West, and South," Hoover said over his shoulder. "Wow, you really ARE bad at directions."

They flew for hours. Eventually, as the hills of the forest below flattened out and the pine trees gave way to maples and oaks, the night sky began to lighten.

"Well, at least it's getting less creepy outside," Speed Bump said. "Hey, Slingshot, let me take a look at that map."

"But—"

"Seriously, we might be getting close, and I don't want us to miss the spot."

"Okay, okay—here."

Slingshot held the map out to his friend. Speed Bump reached to take it, and just as the tip of his wing was on it, a gust of wind sent the map whirling into the sky.

The map danced and darted, then
dipped behind a row of trees.

"Down there!" Soda Pop pointed.
"Behind those oaks!"

Hoover dove back into the forest.
The map had disappeared in the gloom.

"We're at the end of the forest. Where else could it have gone?" Hoover said as they picked through small bushes and poked around old logs.

The three friends plopped down on their tails, leaning against the stump of a fallen tree. Hoover walked over to them.

He looked up at his friend, but
Slingshot was half asleep and making
eating noises.

There was a rumbling sound.

"Slingshot, was that your stomach?"

The rumble got louder. Slingshot leaned over and put his ear near his tummy.

"Nope. Not me."

Suddenly, the tree trunk began to shake. The bushes started rustling, louder and louder. Hoover looked down at his claws.

"What on earth is going on?"

The ground all around them was moving and shifting. Stones bounced and clicked off one another. It was happening as far as they could see,

in the forest and out into the field
beyond.

"I think you mean what UNDER the
earth is going on," Soda Pop yelled.

Hoover jumped onto the tree stump,
and the rest of the friends huddled
around him.

Mounds of dirt began popping up,
some of them almost as big as Speed
Bump and Soda Pop. The echo of mounds
shook and shifted and cast quivering
shadows as the morning sun began
to peek over the distant hill. Then
a cluster of mounds appeared right
in front of them. They all screamed.

RUMBLE RUMBLE

"Something's coming out of the ground!"

"Hoover!" yelled Soda Pop. "Fly us home! Now!"

"I can't feel my wings!" the owl yelled back in a small, terrified voice.

The mounds grew higher and higher. Then the dirt began to fall away, and terrifying creatures appeared. Their hard shells were the color of rusty metal, and six thick, spiky legs stuck out at weird angles from their bodies as they dragged themselves out of the ground. One creature tilted its head up toward them—it had enormous red eyes!

It was the scariest, ugliest thing they'd ever seen.

"ZOMBIE BUGS!" shouted Slingshot. "Don't look into their dead eyes!"

They shuffled in a half circle to face the other way.

"They're on this side, too!"

They shuffled in a quarter circle.

"There are even more over here!"

They shuffled and shuffled and shuffled, like the hands on a clock, but it did no good. They were surrounded by those horrible, bulbous red eyes!

They closed their eyes tight and
braced for the swarm.

CHAPTER SEVEN
SCARED OUT OF THEIR SKIN

The giant insects crawled up the stump and over the friends' claws, pushing against their feathers and fur. They made noises none of them had ever heard. There were clicks and groans and even some chilling scraping noises. It was almost deafening.

But the creatures didn't eat the four friends. They didn't even bite them. In fact, the mob of zombie bugs didn't seem to notice them at all. Instead, they were moving together in one direction, like a river flowing from the field into the forest, their red eyes bobbing along on top.

One by one, the friends opened their eyes.

"We're ALIVE!" Slingshot shouted, checking his body for missing parts. "They didn't even eat one single feather!"

"I think they're leaving us alone," Soda Pop said with a look of relief.

"Oh!" said Hoover. "They're headed for the trees!"

"Why would zombie bugs climb trees?" Soda Pop asked.

"Maybe they're concocting an evil plan!" Speed Bump grimaced.

"Maybe they're going to jump down on top of us!" Slingshot squawked.

"Or maybe," Hoover said thoughtfully, "they're not zombies at all."

They watched as the creatures scratched their way up the tree bark and settled onto branches all around them.

It was as if the bugs were listening, because suddenly they began to get louder and louder and louder.

THREE HOURS LATER
CHIRRR CHIRRR
SNAP SNAP
CLICK CLICK
SNAP SNAP
SNAP
CHIRRRR

Finally Hoover yelled above the din, "Boys, there's only one way to find out if they're zombies or not!"

"What?"

"Ask!"

Before he was even finished with his sentence, Hoover was flying into the forest.

"Wise or not, I think we're safer sticking with him!" Speed Bump flapped his tiny wings and followed as fast as he could.

Soda Pop looked pleadingly at Slingshot.

"Oh, okay, get on my back."

Slingshot groaned as they tried to catch up. "Geez, what did you eat last night? A whole cheese wheel?"

Hoover and Speed Bump were already sitting on a branch when Slingshot and Soda Pop found them. They were peering around the trunk of the tree carefully. On the other side was a zombie bug! It was holding perfectly still.

"Has it seen you? Did you talk to it yet?"

"No! I can't just say, 'Hey, you're really ugly. Are you a zombie?' That would be rude."

"Zombies care about manners?"

"Well, I don't want to make it mad. Do you?"

They waited, glancing around nervously. A few minutes went by. Finally, Soda Pop cleared his throat and gave Hoover a look that said, "Well?"

"All right, all right, here I go!" Hoover said.

He took one big step onto a branch and leaned closer to the bug.

Then he screamed.

He screamed so loud that Speed Bump fell off the branch, which made Soda Pop burp so hard that he also fell. Fortunately, Slingshot was able to grab his long tail and pull him back up.

They jumped to the next branch to see what was going on. Then they all screamed, too. Slingshot looked queasy and fainted against the tree.

THE BACK OF THE
ZOMBIE BUG WAS
SPLITTING OPEN AND
A **NEW** ZOMBIE BUG
WAS COMING OUT!

"I think I'm going to be sick," Speed Bump said.

But none of them could take their eyes off what was happening. A triangle-shaped head came out of the shell first, and its eyes were just as red as the old ones. One brown leg pushed its way out, then another. It clamped on to the tree, and with a few more pulls, the whole new bug appeared, green and shiny.

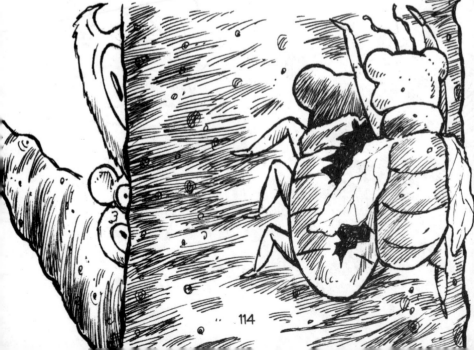

"Oh, great, it has WINGS!" Soda Pop muttered. "THIS just went from bad to worse. Now the zombie bugs can FLY."

"Oh no! It's happening to the others, too!" Soda Pop squeaked.

Bugs were emerging from the skins of their old bodies on the other trees as well. Some of them were already flying, zipping by the friends' heads and making such a ruckus that they could hardly hear themselves think.

Slingshot woke up, took one look at the zombie bug hovering in front of his face, and fainted again.

They turned back to the bug. The skin it had crawled out of was still stuck to the tree, but it was transparent and empty. The new bug was shaking its wings, as if to dry them. It slowly rotated its head toward them, and its eyes seemed to get even bigger. They all stared at one another.

Then the zombie bug

SHRIEKED.

CHAPTER EIGHT
ZOMBIE LOVE

The zombie bug's shriek made Speed Bump, Soda Pop, and Hoover scream again. Which made the bug shriek again. Which made *them* scream again. They took turns shrieking and screaming for a minute until Slingshot finally woke up.

"Oh, wow, I just had the WEIRDEST dream, you guys! We were in this forest, and there were these crazy bugs, but they weren't really bugs because they were DEAD, but they still LOOKED like bugs, and...and...uh-oh."

Everyone was now staring at
Slingshot, including the bug. To their
surprise, the bug spoke.

Please,
Please,
PLEASE
don't eat
me!

"I know you eat bugs. I get it—it's
what you do. It's not your fault. But
listen, I've been underground seventeen
years. SEVENTEEN YEARS! I've been
waiting for this moment for, like, a
really, really long time."

The four friends were speechless for a moment. Then Slingshot said, "Soooo . . . you're NOT a zombie?"

"A WHAT? A ZOMBIE? Nope. I've been alive and well underground, just doing my thing. You know, 'underground' stuff—digging tunnels, chillin' with the other 'cadas, digging more tunnels, playing guessing games about what's above all the dirt. Did I mention chillin'? Lots of chillin'."

Soda Pop looked at his friends. "He seems...nice."

"We thought you were going to eat US," said Speed Bump.

"I thought YOU were going to eat ME," said the bug.

Slingshot drooled a little bit. "Don't even think about it," Speed Bump whispered.

"But since you're NOT going to eat me, let me introduce myself. I'm Collin."

"Speed Bump."

"Slingshot."

"Soda Pop."

"Hoover. And by the way, what's a ''cada'?"

"Oh, yeah, that's just short for CICADA. All these dudes and dudettes that you see flying around here, they're cicadas. They might seem a little loud and crazy, but if you were born under the dirt and had never been outside, you'd be pretty boisterous yourself right about now!"

"Interesting. I guess you can learn something new every day," said Hoover, "even a wise old owl like me."

Speed Bump's eyes lit up as he thought of an idea. "So, Collin, you've been underground your whole life. Why don't you come with us? We can show you all the stuff you've never seen, like bullfrogs and telephone wires and raccoons and—"

"We could take him to the MALL!" Slingshot said.

They paused and looked at one another.

"Okay, maybe not the mall."

"That's a fantastic offer, guys, really, but there's something super important I must do here."

Collin shut his eyes. Then he started squishing his stomach in and out, in and out, until his body screeched so loud they had to cover their ears.

"Pretty cool, huh? That's my mating call. I have a job to do, and that's find another cicada to make baby 'cadas with, and then we'll put those eggs in the ground. If you come back in seventeen years when the eggs hatch, you can meet my kids!"

And with that, he buzzed off, quickly blending in with the thousands of other cicadas in the noisy forest.

CHAPTER NINE
AMIS POUR TOUJOURS*

*friends forever

Hoover whistled. "I'm sure I speak for all of us when I say: That's enough excitement for one morning."

As the rest of them yawned and nodded, they heard something crunching behind them. They turned to see Slingshot happily munching on the hollow old cicada skin.

"Uh, no." Soda Pop looked puzzled. "Is it any good?"

"Yeah, actually, it's not bad, not bad at all. But I'll tell you what," Slingshot continued, "I'm going to be hungry again in an hour."

Soda Pop climbed on Hoover's back. "You two know how to get home, don't you?"

"Yeah," said Slingshot. "We just head toward N, right? Or is it S? E? W, maybe?"

The mouse just blinked.

"I'm KIDDING. Yes, we know."

With a wave and one last burp, Hoover and Soda Pop headed up into the morning sky. Speed Bump and Slingshot rose out of the cloud of cicadas, too, enjoying the quiet as they flew above the forest and back toward their own nests.

They flew on in silence for a bit.

"I know what you're thinking," Speed Bump said eventually.

"What's that?"

"You're secretly disappointed that they weren't zombies."

"You know me too well."

"It doesn't make any sense, but you know what? I kind of am, too."

"It's okay," Slingshot said. "Those bugs may not have been zombies, but the old rook was right about one thing."

"Oh yeah, what's that?"

TRUE CICADA FACTS

*The scientific name for the seventeen-year cicadas is Magicicada

*Cicadas think power tools, such as lawn mowers, sound like other cicadas, and will swarm around when they hear them.

*Cicadas actually have five eyes! They have two large eyes, of course, but they also have three tiny eyes called "ocelli", which are between the two large ones.

*Cicadas that come out of the ground before they are supposed to are called "stragglers."

*Did you know that cicadas pee? They drink tree fluids, so they have to "go" just like people do. Some people call it "honey dew" or "cicada rain."

NOT·SO·TRUE CICADA FACTS

*If you put an old cicada skin between two graham crackers, then add a Hershey bar and a melted marshmallow, it's called a "s'cada." They're delicious!

*Ninety-seven percent of cicadas make a screeching noise to attract a mate, but the other three percent don't care if they find a mate. They just screech to be annoying.

*Some cicadas never come out of the ground. They prefer to stay inside and play video games for another 17 years. It drives their moms crazy.

*The largest cicada ever found was four feet long and discovered by the Gardner family on their farm in Plainwell, Michigan. All twelve of the Gardner children wore the old hollow skin as a Halloween costume at one time or another.

*Did you know a cicada ran for president in 1888? Henry "Crusty" McHairy was actually leading in the polls, until it was discovered that Henry's running mate for vice president, Chester "Stinky" Burrows, was actually a dung beetle.